MEET

O.C.
THE

SUPERSTARS

The Official Biography!

As Told to Monica Rizzo

SCHOLASTIC INC.

New York   Toronto   London   Auckland   Sydney
Mexico City   New Delhi   Hong Kong   Buenos Aires

ISBN 0-439-66060-2

Designed by Louise Bova

12 11 10 9 8 7 6 5 4 3 2 1   4 5 6 7 8 9 10

Printed in the U.S.A.
First printing, May 2004

MEET The O.C. SUPERSTARS

THE OFFICIAL BIOGRAPHY OF TV'S NEWEST MEGASTARS!

HERE'S WHAT — AND WHO — YOU NEED TO KNOW!

THE O.C. IS...
...MUST-SEE
...TV!

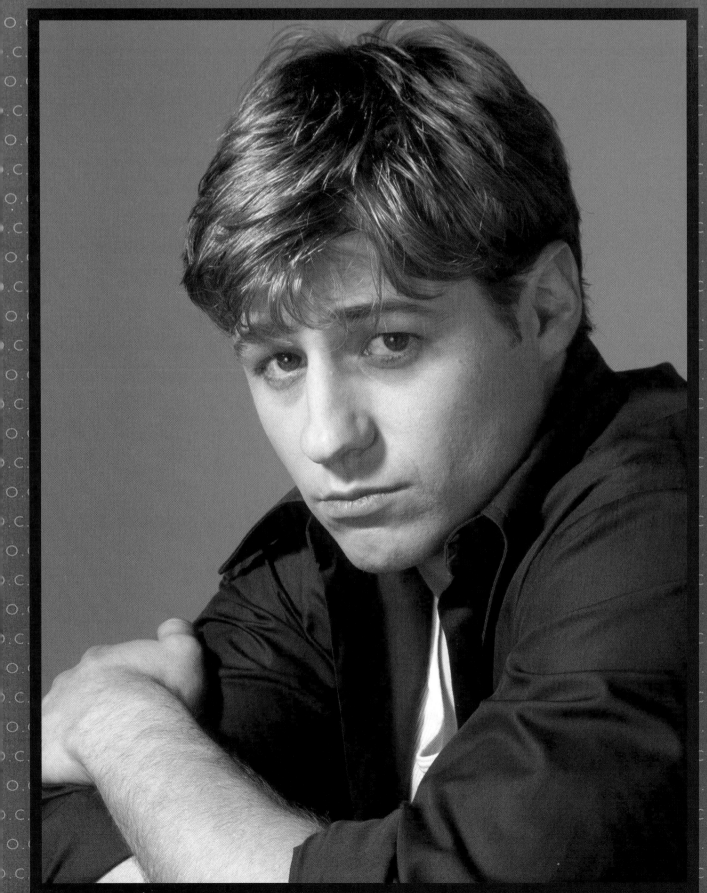

BENJAMIN MCKENZIE
"RYAN ATWOOD"

Ryan Atwood is the new kid in town and he is played by actor Benjamin McKenzie.

Everything that happens in *The O.C.* — good, bad, pretty, and the pretty ugly — gets amped up upon Ryan's arrival. He's the catalyst, the linchpin for the show and all its characters.

Ryan spent the first 16 years of his life in the small working-class town of Chino, California. His childhood was trouble-filled from day one: Call it *"8 Mile*, Chino style." Dad's in prison; delinquent older bro Trey's on the way there; Mom suffers from alcoholism and has bad taste in boyfriends (one of them punched out Ryan in the show's pilot). She added insult to assault by abandoning him altogether.

Ryan always had the smarts and sensitivity for a better life, only not the means. That was taken care of when, courtesy of Trey, he landed in juvie for stealing a car and met do-good lawyer Sandy Cohen, who took him home — to his oceanfront mansion, breadwinner wife, Kirsten, and lonely only son, Seth . . . to Orange County, *The O.C.*

Cue the "fish out of water" plotline.

Cue newcomer Benjamin McKenzie for breathing life into Ryan. His take: "Ryan is fundamentally good but also, because of his past, has problems; he is very distrustful of people. He can be violent and he has problems controlling his anger and controlling his tongue. He is kind of lost; initially when we start the show he's very fragile in a way. He doesn't want to admit it and tries to hide it the best he can."

Peter Gallagher, Mischa Barton, and Ben McKenzie star as The O.C.'s **Sandy, Marissa, and Ryan.**

5

One thing that sets Ryan apart from the often-portrayed brooding, leather-jacket-wearing bad boy is that he really wants to succeed in life and he is grateful for the opportunity the Cohens have given him. "We're able to have Ryan be incredibly strong and stoic yet utterly fragile which hopefully creates a very compelling character to watch," Ben says.

Ryan discovers that the world has a lot to offer him so long as he puts forth the effort. That is very similar to the lessons Ben learned when he was growing up.

Ben's Boyhood:
Deep in the Heart of Texas

Benjamin McKenzie Schenkkan is the oldest of three children. He was born and raised in Austin, Texas. His growing-up years were about as far from his character's as you can get. Ben's dad, Pete, is an attorney, and mom, Frances, is a poet/writer. Ben's brothers are Nate, 22, an actor, and Zack, 19, a college student.

Ben's boyhood is filled with many fond memories. "I had two very loving parents. Austin was a very relaxed, quiet kind of town and I had a very sweet and wonderful childhood," describes Ben, noting that at times he took advantage of being the oldest boy in his family.

Ben bonded easily with Adam Brody, who plays Seth.

Seth is a frequent "guest" in Ryan's pool-house crib.

"Don't ask my younger brothers how loving I was. We were always beating up each other, wrestling and boxing around — typical boy stuff. I beat up Nate on so many occasions," Ben says, laughing. "I think he's remarkably well-adjusted considering the torture I put him through back then."

When Ben was in junior high and high school he lightened up on his younger brother and instead focused his energy on football. Yes, Ben (more like *The O.C.*'s Luke than Ryan) was a jock! He played wide receiver and defensive back for the Austin High Maroon football team and scored his fair share of touchdowns. Football was the one sport he loved more than anything.

"Football is a religion down there in Texas. We practiced hard and played hard and had a good time doing it," says Ben.

Ben was an outstanding team member and enjoyed practicing and playing ball with his friends, but he often enjoyed time to himself so he could read and study. "I was never one to seek out the popular kids in school. I studied a lot and generally just kept to myself. I've always been a quiet type, not enormously socially aggressive."

Courage was in short supply, however, when it came to the school's drama club. He never joined. "I guess I didn't have the guts then," he admits. That was surprising because theater runs in the Schenkkan family. Ben's uncle Robert Schenkkan is an actor and a Pulitzer

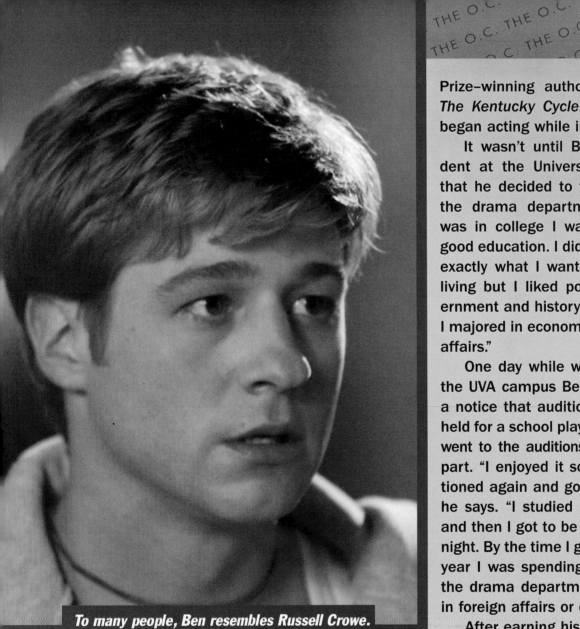

To many people, Ben resembles Russell Crowe.

Prize–winning author of the play *The Kentucky Cycle*. Brother Nate began acting while in high school.

It wasn't until Ben was a student at the University of Virginia that he decided to take a look at the drama department. "When I was in college I wanted to get a good education. I didn't really know exactly what I wanted to do for a living but I liked politics and government and history and literature. I majored in economics and foreign affairs."

One day while walking through the UVA campus Ben came across a notice that auditions were being held for a school play. On a lark Ben went to the auditions and landed a part. "I enjoyed it so much, I auditioned again and got another one," he says. "I studied during the day and then I got to be a little artsy at night. By the time I got to my fourth year I was spending more time in the drama department than I was in foreign affairs or economics."

After earning his degree in May 2001 Ben held off looking for a job in his major and decided instead to take a shot at becoming a professional actor. "I thought, 'Hey, what do I have to lose?' It was the only time in my life where I had the fewest obligations — not married, no kids, no huge college tuition bills to pay off."

He apprenticed at the Williamstown Theater Festival that summer in Williamstown, Massachusetts. Every year the world's top actors travel to the festival, which is one of the most respected gatherings in the theater world, drawing talent such as Gwyneth Paltrow and Ethan Hawke. During the summer Ben attended the festival, he was able to observe and learn from experienced actors like Sam Rockwell.

At the end of the summer he moved to New York City with a couple of friends. Three guys crammed into a tiny two-bedroom apartment near the city's theater district. Just as Ben was getting settled into his new digs, the September 11 terrorist attacks occurred.

"It was a very strange time to be there," he notes. The tragedy affected everyone, Ben included. "It made me question what I was doing. It felt so frivolous to be acting."

In the end, Ben stuck it out and paid his dues like many aspiring actors. He waited tables and eventually began to land small roles in Off-Off-Broadway plays. A friend introduced him to a theatrical agent, who suggested Ben go to Los Angeles to meet with his West Coast counterpart. The agent thought his partner might be able to help Ben break into television acting. Ben packed his bags in April 2002 for what he thought would be a one-week trip.

It's been a looooong week!

Bad Boy in the City of Angels

Ben found a small but affordable apartment in the San Fernando Valley area of Los Angeles. After months of try-

Ben has many scenes with Mischa Barton. Good thing they're friends off-camera, too.

ing to just get the chance to audition, he landed a two-line voice-over part in a Dr Pepper commercial and later a guest-starring role on TV's *JAG*. One year and countless auditions later, Ben landed his breakthrough role — Ryan Atwood on *The O.C.*

"I knew this was a good show and I knew I had auditioned as well as I could," says Ben, who compares getting the role of Ryan to "hitting the lottery."

It couldn't have happened at a better time. Like all actors who are at the beginning stages of their careers, Ben was trying to work several jobs in order to pay his rent and bills, and in his free time pursue acting work. Because a lot of auditions happen during the day, Ben needed a flexible work schedule. He sold tickets at the Mark Taper Forum, a performing arts center in downtown Los Angeles, and, as he had done in New York, he waited tables at a small restaurant.

"I wasn't a very good waiter," Ben says, laughing. "I had customers complain and constantly tell me I was terrible. Here I was living in the Valley, driving in an un-air-conditioned car from audition to audition getting rejected over and over, then I'd go to my night job where

I had to work to pay the bills. It was a period of struggle but I know I'm blessed to have reached success as fast as I have."

When Ben walked into the audition room where *O.C.* producers Josh Schwartz and McG were sitting, he figured he'd act the part the way *he* wanted to and not the way he thought they might want him to. "I didn't try to impress anybody, which was different from my other auditions and I think that's why I got it," Ben says.

He had a comfort level with the role because he and Ryan have a few things in common. "I don't think I'm brooding like Ryan, but I am a bit of a loner, contemplative. I'm friendly and nice but I'm not a gregarious type of person. That may be what the producers picked up on."

How are Ben and Ryan different? Well, Ben says, "We have completely different backgrounds. I came from such a loving family." When it comes to girls, Ben says Ryan is much more of a ladies' man. "I dated a few girls in high school but I was too nervous at that point to really like girls. I still am."

As for his *O.C.* costar Mischa Barton, Ben says, "She's cool." What's not cool is when Ryan and Marissa have a kissing scene. There's nothing romantic or private about it at all, Ben says. "Kissing someone for a job is just strange — having a hundred people watching you, but they're really not watching for you, they just need to see if the lighting's right or the sound's right, so they have to look at you."

Fans can't get enough of scenes like this!

"*The character I'm playing is different and fresh. Just seeing the conflict of him trying at all times to do the right thing, and yet despite that being held back and criticized and blamed for things outside of his control makes for a very sweet show where you're hopefully rooting for all the characters, not just Ryan.*"

After getting the role Ben decided to do a bit of research. He jumped in his car and drove to Orange County and Ryan's hometown of Chino. "It's a perfectly lovely town. Like anyplace, it has nice parts and probably not-so-nice parts, which is where they imagine Ryan is from," Ben says.

Both places, Ben says, are a world away from his hometown of Austin. When Ben first moved to Los Angeles, he felt a little bit like Ryan in ritzy Newport Beach. "I felt a little bit like a fish out of water. L.A. is full of fabulous wealth and odd people behaving oddly."

After a two-year adjustment period, Ben has settled nicely into the cozy beach community of Santa Monica, where he rents an apartment. In his free time Ben enjoys reading, watching movies, going to the gym, and running at the beach. Weekends are spent watching football games and playing in an entertainment basketball league with his *O.C.* costars Chris Carmack (Luke) and Adam Brody (Seth). Occasionally, Ben gets a little nostalgic for his hometown.

"I feel closer to things from Texas now that I've left and I guess it's because I kind of cling to things that remind myself of where I'm from. I wear cowboy boots. I listen to country music like Johnny Cash, Lyle Lovett, and Willie Nelson," Ben says.

Still, California has taken hold on Ben, who can't deny that there's no place he'd rather be. "I'm glad things happened the way they did. I'm on a show that I'm really proud of."

Almost Famous

When Ben got to Los Angeles he discovered that there was already a working actor by the name of Ben Schenkman. Because their names were so similar and because the other Ben was already known in the entertainment industry (he starred in the HBO movie *Angels in America*), Ben decided to use McKenzie, his middle name, as his last name for his acting credits.

It only took one airing of *The O.C.* in August 2003 for people to connect to Ben. While he usually values his alone time, Ben is slowly adjusting to getting recognized wherever he goes. "People are so supportive. Sometimes it's a little kid and then it's someone's grandmother. One of my friends asked me to sign a picture for his grandmother to give her for Christmas. I can't think of a lot of other shows that would have that broad appeal," Ben says.

Ben isn't the only one who's been affected by the success of *The O.C.* His parents back in Texas receive lots of fan mail and gifts for him. "There was this woman who sent me pillowcases that she had sewn. She sent them to me at my family's home address in Texas. I don't know who she is," Ben says of the fan. "It's pretty strange, but it's pretty flattering."

Going from being just another customer in line at the supermarket to a superstar on the covers of magazines like *TV Guide* and *Entertainment Weekly* — which are sold in the supermarket! — is a little bit trippy. But Ben swears he's not letting it get to his head. He still waits his turn in line when he's at the store, and he still prefers quiet evenings at home reading a book or hanging out with a couple of friends. "I'm not really into going to parties. I went to the premiere of *Grind* because Adam [Brody, who plays Seth

Cohen on *The O.C.]* was in it, and I've gone to things for publicity for the show, but that's about it," Ben asserts.

When he's working, Ben usually eats on the run, which is sometimes takeout or the catered meals *The O.C.* set provides for the actors when they have to work long hours. When he has the time, Ben loves to cook chili, pasta, and chicken dishes. He also cleans his apartment without the help of a maid and does his own laundry.

Ben's social life doesn't include a special someone right now. He dates and says there are qualities he admires in a girl. "I like someone ambitious, who is driven and passionate about whatever it is they want to do," Ben says. "I like people who are going to do something with their lives rather than just talk about it."

There's a lot of buzz about Ben, who's one of Hollywood's most sought-after young actors. In 2003 *People* magazine named Ben one of its sexiest men and *Entertainment Weekly* proclaimed him and his *O.C.* castmates TV's breakout stars of the year. He's being pursued for numerous film roles, which is a bit overwhelming for a guy who just a year ago was wearing an apron and taking orders from demanding customers. Life has changed for Ben since *The O.C.* took off, but he swears he's still the same guy he was growing up in Texas.

"I have a pretty good sense of who I am and I think I'm pretty good at sticking to what I believe in," Ben says. "Success doesn't change who you are."

ADAM BRODY
"SETH COHEN"

Adam Brody plays quirky, quippy, sensitive Seth Cohen, the only child of lawyer Sandy and real estate developer Kirstin Cohen. At his status-conscious high school, Seth's an enigma — neither jock nor brain, he's not part of the popular crowd (nor would he want to be) but he's far from an outcast. Even "geek" is an unfair tag. No one knows quite what to make of him, since Seth defies stereotyping. Yet sweet, smart Seth oozes an infectious warmth and sincerity that makes him extremely likable.

And brave. Like his O.C. dad, Sandy, Seth is perceptive — he sees beyond the superficiality, behind the masks people wear to protect themselves.

Seth is vulnerable and unafraid to let others see the real him.

Adam Brody has this take on his character: "Seth doesn't necessarily go with the flow of his school, but if he grew up in New York he'd be one of the most popular kids. I've always seen him on the outside of this bubble but it's by choice more than it is them not letting him in. If he just put on the clothes and walked the walk he might fit in better but he doesn't want to."

Turned out he didn't have to.

The O.C.'s first season has been one of victory and vindication for Seth

A new family — Sandy and Kirstin, played by Peter Gallagher and Kelly Rowan, have their own issues, but the pair make cool 'rents for Seth and Ryan.

15

Seth is Summer's good luck charm at the for-charity gaming table — but is she good for him? That was his quandary in season one!

Cohen. He began as the boy with all the material toys — a backyard swimming pool, an SUV, the latest in laptops and PlayStations — but precious little of what he really needed: friendship, acceptance, and the attention of the girl he pined for.

By season's end, he had all that and more. Ryan became his best friend, and hottie-next-door Marissa, a bonus bud. The chilly Summer, ice princess of his dreams, fell for him. New girl at school Anna did, too — a bonus babe. He gained the grudging respect, and acceptance even, of the Harbor High kids.

Best of all? Seth accomplished all that without having to "fit in."

Adam Brody isn't so very different from Seth Cohen. And that, as you'll see, is a very good thing!

SK8TR Boy

Adam Jared Brody was born on December 15, 1979, in San Diego, California. He's the oldest of three boys raised by Mark, an attorney, and Valerie, a graphic artist. Adam has younger twin brothers, Sean and Matt, who are 19 and currently attend college.

When Adam was very young his family moved to a San Diego suburb called Scripps Ranch, not nearly so posh as his *O.C.* digs, but "It was a great place to grow up," Adam says. "We had a nice big yard and it was a safe suburb."

Early on, Adam played baseball and soccer, rode his bike, and skateboarded all around the neighborhood. But his favorite game was playing *Teenage Mutant Ninja Turtles* with his friends.

"That was the ultimate," Adam enthuses. "I was Raphael. I liked him because he was the lead in the movie. But now I realize looking back on it that he was kind of a jerk and had kind of an attitude. I'd rather be Michelangelo because he knew how to chill and have fun."

Adam gives his mom props for allowing him space — and tools — to nurture his imagination, a trait that comes in very handy as an actor. "She was very cool. At the time it made me so mad because she wouldn't let us play with toy guns or swords or anything and all I wanted to play was *Young Guns* or *Ninja Turtles*," Adam explains. "I was so pissed. But my mom had tons and tons of paper around because of her job, so me and my two brothers would make GI Joe guns out of rolls of paper taped together. The homemade stuff was a pain at the time but I look back on it now and I think it was such a great thing my mom did in not sponsoring violence."

While a student at Scripps Ranch High School, Adam often let other interests get in the way of his schoolwork. "I started surfing in sixth grade and seriously got into it in ninth grade. It was all I wanted to do," Adam says. "I didn't apply myself to school but I had the smarts. English and history class were great. If I did it again I'd take much more of an interest in it, though math would still bore the crap out of me."

At age 18 Adam graduated from high school, but he had no idea what he wanted to do with his life. His father encouraged him to go to college, but Adam resisted. "I told my dad, 'You know what? I don't know what I want to do yet and I don't want to waste your money,'" Adam explains. As a compromise Adam enrolled in Mira Costa Community College, where he could take a few classes, work part-time, and surf. "I got this job at Blockbuster and I was, like, 'I'll go to school for my classes, surf every day, work, and life will be fantastic. It sounded great until two weeks after that life started. It was so boring. I was working at Blockbuster and kept thinking I wanted to try something else. Working around all those movies all day got me interested in movies."

On a whim, Adam and a friend drove north two hours to Los Angeles. Adam's friend knew a guy

who was just getting started in acting and had appeared in an episode of *Power Rangers*. "I thought it was the biggest thing ever," Adam says.

The young actor told Adam that many newcomers begin their careers by being "extras." An extra is an actor who usually appears in the background of a scene and doesn't have any lines. The thought of just being on a movie set excited Adam so much, he just had to give it a try. He gave himself a six-month deadline.

"I thought if I could move to L.A., be a waiter, do an acting class and maybe a student film once in a while, and maybe once in a blue moon do a commercial, I would be the happiest man in the world," Adam says.

Adam waited tables at Damiano's Pizza and parked cars at the Beverly Hills Hotel. He stayed in a supersmall apartment in Santa Monica. "The first year in L.A. was the loneliest year of my life. Me and my roommate shared this little L-shaped studio apartment. We had bunk beds and there was one desk and one chair, so only one person could be sitting at a time or eating at a time. You couldn't sit on the beds because your head would either hit the

Seth Cohen, hottie? Maybe that IS how they do it in The OC!

ceiling or hit the other bunk bed."

Then one day he got a major break. "There was this coffee shop scene on *The Young and the Restless* with the two main characters. They were eating and I'm at a table with some extras and I get up and say some lines to one of the leads and then go sit back down," Adam explains. "So here I am sitting at this table talking about extra stuff with the other actors, then I get up, do my lines, and sit back down and literally, the expressions on their faces — you'd have thought I ripped off my clothes and was wearing a Superman outfit. It was so cool!"

Geek Chic

The cool stuff didn't end there. Adam went on to star as Greg Brady in the TV movie *Growing Up Brady.* The behind-the-scenes look at the popular 70s television show was truly a big break for Adam. From that point on, he was able to give up all of the odd jobs and

Along came Anna — who fell for Seth. "He's a bit cocky," Adam says of Seth's newfound magnetism. "He's pretty dry and a smart aleck about it."

just concentrate on his acting career. Adam was thrilled to be a steadily employed actor in Hollywood. He moved out of his cramped Santa Monica studio apartment and into a much more spacious place of his own in Hollywood. He landed guest-starring roles on critically acclaimed TV shows like *Once and Again, Judging Amy,* and *Family Law,* and a lead role as Lucas in *MTV's Undressed.* He also had small roles in big films like *American Pie 2* and *The Ring.*

In the 2002–2003 season of *Gilmore Girls,* Adam's acting profile was raised when he appeared for nine episodes as Lane's boyfriend Dave on the hit WB show. Adam also landed a lead role in *Grind,* a feature film about four skateboarders trying to make it big.

Hollywood stars, Adam found out, can come in different shapes and sizes. His own long, lanky physique isn't that of the typical primetime hottie. But he's proof that qualities other than six-pack abs and bulging biceps can also make a heartthrob. He's the thinking girl's kind of guy. He's read a few books, seen a few movies, and had his heart broken on more than one occasion. He's exactly the kind of guy the creators of *The O.C.* were looking for when they set out to cast the role of Seth.

Adam was immediately attracted to the show because two of his favorite people — director Doug Liman and producer McG — were working on it. He figured if they were involved in the project then it must be good. His hunch was right.

When Adam auditioned he did something most actors don't — he began ad-libbing some of his lines. Normally the actor is brought in and asked to read the dialogue exactly as it's written. Adam decided to spice things up and inject his own personality into the character. At first the producers were a bit wary of this bold tactic. But Adam wasn't trying to be disrespectful, he was just trying to give the character more of a personality. It worked. Adam was asked to come back for a second meeting. This time his ad-libbing was embraced. The producers liked that Adam had the insight and the confidence to see a more well-rounded character in Seth and thus, he got the job.

Sometimes, Adam says, "It's hard for people to tell the difference between fact and fiction. Sometimes the other cast members ask if I'm dressed when we're rehearsing the scene." Adam notes that he and Seth tend to wear the same kind of clothing — jeans, Nike sneakers, vintage T-shirts, and short-sleeve button-down oxford shirts. "He's got his own style, his own flavor, his own opinions. He's not totally mainstream. He's definitely not listening to Top 40 music and I love that about him."

Another big similarity between Seth and Adam is their taste in music. Adam's biggest pet peeve is Top 40 stations. "I can't stand pop music. I'm much more a fan of independent bands like Bright Eyes," he says, noting that another of his favorite bands, Death Cab for Cutie, was mentioned on the

Ryan, who was abandoned by his family, has a lot of qualities Seth wishes he had, like good looks, a muscled body, a storied past. Little does Seth know that he has many things Ryan would dream of, like two loving parents, a nice home with a warm bed, a good education, a solid future.

show in a scene where Seth gives a CD of theirs to Anna and Summer.

How are Adam and Seth different? "I like to think I'm a little steadier on my feet with girls. I'm not very technologically savvy," the actor admits. "I play video games once in a while, but not like Seth. I just got a laptop computer like six months ago and I am just now learning how to surf the Internet."

Speaking of surfing, Adam's board has been gathering a little dust since his career has taken off. He still goes, he says, when he visits with his family in San Diego. He misses hanging at the beach, but for now the artificial Orange County sand and water backdrops will have to suffice. But Adam's not complaining. "When I first moved to L.A., I had no goal of being where I am now," he says. "Acting turned out to be something I love. I really feel it is my calling."

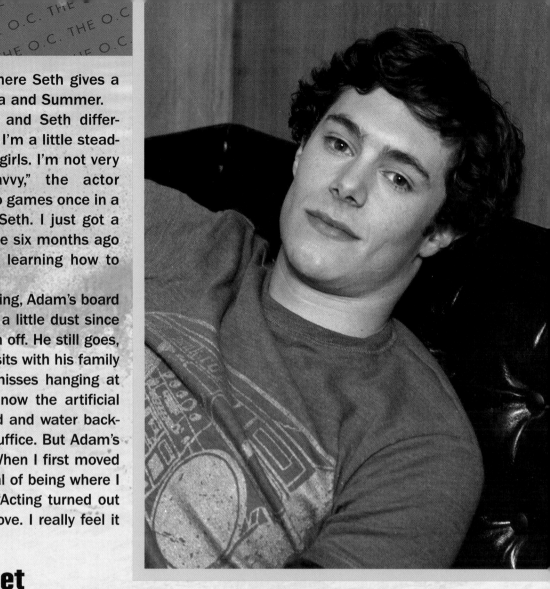

Chick Magnet

Adam has definitely found himself the center of attention since landing on *The O.C.* Practically everywhere he goes these days he gets recognized. "It's like it's gone from zero to sixty," Adam says. "First it was 'Hey, *The O.C.* dude!' Then it was 'Hey, Seth Cohen.' Now it's 'Hey, Adam Brody!', mostly from the teenage girls. It's cool, though."

When Adam isn't working he often spends his time reading or going to movies, or playing on an entertainment basketball team with costars Ben McKenzie and Chris Carmack. "Weekends are for friends," says Adam, who likes to get a small group together and head over to Canter's Deli for a sandwich.

Adam confesses there's practically no food he doesn't enjoy, and practically no food he knows how to prepare. "I really don't cook. I eat a lot of meals out. The hardest thing I ever made was an omelet once. I have never made meat. I have never grilled," he admits.

Instead Adam goes out a lot. He likes to go to places where there's choice people-watching, like The Farmer's Market and The Grove, a mall in Los Angeles.

Occasionally, Adam likes to chill out on his own. He remembers his early days in Los Angeles when he barely knew a soul. He'd grab his skateboard (how very Seth Cohen!) and

head down to the Third Street Promenade shopping area in Santa Monica where there are movie theaters, restaurants, and stores. "I'd skate down there all the time and see movies by myself. I have fond memories of discovery," Adam says.

When it comes to dating, Adam prefers girls who have a cool, funky style. On the show, Seth was torn between fashion-forward Summer and fashion-funky Anna. In real life, Adam says the choice would be a bit easier. "I'd go for an Anna type. But the truth of the matter is sometimes you go out with the Anna and the Anna is in love with you and you wish you could swallow a pill and be in love with her. Then there's the Summers in the world where you're, like, man, on paper I don't like this person but when it comes down to it you really can't help [liking her]."

But someone who wears Prada might actually be a turn-off. "I like it when girls have their own style, their own flavor. I also don't like girls with little dogs that they carry around in their purse," Adam says, noting, "I love animals. But it doesn't count as a dog if you can carry it in your purse."

Adam's sense of humor

and sincere modesty transcend onto the screen. He's been compared to a young Tom Hanks because he's got boy-next-door good looks, he's funny, and he's passionate about his work. Adam shrugs off the comparison and praise and instead applauds his costar Ben McKenzie. "As soon as I met Ben, I thought it was the smartest thing they did, to cast him. I really think Ben is a key to the show. I feel like the credit I get for my character is undeserved. A lot of people have responded really well to my character. I feel like it's not so much me as it is the nature of my character — he's free to run around and make jokes. I don't have that heavy of a burden to bear."

Indeed, Adam's biggest "burden" is fielding the many phone calls that are coming his way now that The O.C. is a huge success. He enjoyed making Grind and hopes to do another movie when the series goes on hiatus for the summer.

It took five years for Adam to get to where he is and he couldn't be prouder. Still, he says, "I sometimes go back to the Promenade and pretend I'm that guy nobody knows, but it's a little bit tough. I put my head down if we're walking by a group of girls.

"I've had fans freak out, actually semi-hyperventilate. What's so weird is that literally months ago I could have served them at Denny's and they wouldn't have batted an eye."

MISCHA BARTON
"MARISSA COOPER"

Mischa Barton plays 16-year-old Marissa Cooper on *The O.C.* When we first meet Marissa, she is a girl who seems to have it all. Her family is wealthy, she drives a hot new SUV, she's invited to all the cool parties in town, and she wears the greatest clothes money can buy. She's on many organizing committees at the Harbor School, where she's totally popular, and she dates Luke Ward, the hot school jock and Newport Beach golden boy. Together the two of them look like they belong in an Abercrombie and Fitch catalog.

Marissa's life seems like perfection on a posh platter.

Of course, nothing is ever as it seems — what a boring TV show that would make! In reality, this TV teen princess has challenges and struggles like everybody else. Okay, ramp that up: like everybody else on TV!

Mischa, the real-life actress who plays Marissa, agrees. "Marissa is described as the girl next door and I think initially when the show started she was set up to be this perfect girl who every boy would dream about. She's got this wonderful facade of beautiful clothing and every-thing going right and a rich family. And then you look beneath that cover and you

Marissa's TV bff is Summer, who is played by Rachel Bilson.

realize she's a self-conscious, rebellious, not-very-happy-with-her-family girl."

Over the course of *The O.C.*'s first season, Marissa was on angst-overload. Dad lost all their money; Mom told Dad to get lost; her boyfriend cheated on her; she overdosed — and she fell hard for the wildly unacceptable boy from Chino, Ryan Atwood.

That didn't go very well, either.

Marissa Cooper could have seemed like a two-dimensional "poor little rich girl" stereotype. It's because of actress Mischa Barton that she comes across as real, someone audiences believe in and root for.

Mischa's a Real-Life New York City Girl

Mischa was born on January 24, 1986, in London, England, to Paul, a stockbroker, and Nula, a former photographer. She is the second of three children — all girls — in her family. Her older sister, Zoe, is now 26, and her younger sister, Hania, is 15.

Because of her father's job, Mischa's family moved often. Before she was four years old she had lived in several European countries, including France, Germany, Switzerland, and England. When she was five, her father decided to take a job in New York City. The family moved again, but this time it was for good. They settled into a lower Manhattan neighborhood located near the city's financial district.

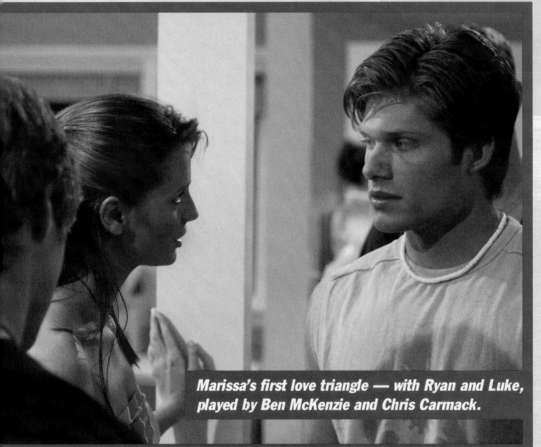

Marissa's first love triangle — with Ryan and Luke, played by Ben McKenzie and Chris Carmack.

At an early age Mischa discovered she was a bit different from other kids her age. "I didn't fit in with the public school system in New York. I had no friends and I really was an outsider." She describes herself back then as "tomboy dorky. I had thick glasses and overalls."

Unlike other kids who got together to watch television or play video games, Mischa preferred to stay at home and read and write. "I was so into literature. It was all I wanted to do."

When Mischa was eight, she and Zoe attended a summer camp in Pennsylvania. Mischa's parents instructed Zoe to look after her younger sister and make sure she participated in things. Only that didn't exactly happen. As Mischa recalls, "It was such a typical older sister thing. All she did all summer was go horseback riding and hang out with her friends and totally ignore me, the younger sister she was supposed to be taking care of."

As it turned out, that was the best thing that ever could have happened to Mischa. While Zoe went off and did things that she liked, Mischa found a camp activity that suited her interests. "There was a writing course and all we had to do was go in and brainstorm every day and write a piece from our imaginations. I wrote a monologue about turtles and then at the end of camp we all performed them in a show — kind of like a play — for our parents.

This is the Ferris wheel scene — a minute later, they shared their first kiss.

"I was putting on my little monologue and an agent came up to my mom and said I should really try auditioning for plays because he thought I had good stage presence," Mischa says. "I remember thinking that I had such a crappy summer camp experience and here in the end it turned out to be all right."

When the family returned to New York, Mischa auditioned for and landed a lead role as a young girl named Emma in *Slavs!*, a Broadway play about life in the Soviet Union (now known as Russia). The play was a big hit and Mischa soon began her life as a working kid actress in New York City.

All My Children, one of the most popular soap operas on television, tapped Mischa, then age nine, to play a young autistic girl named Lilly Montgomery. It was a steady gig for Mischa, who was totally stoked. But it also meant that her schoolwork suffered since she couldn't devote as much time to it as necessary, which didn't go over very well at the public school she'd been attending. It didn't help that one of her teachers strongly disapproved of students who pursue acting careers.

Most importantly, Mischa herself was upset about it.

"My grades started slipping and that was something I didn't want to happen because I

Mischa's relationship with her own mom is the opposite of Marissa and Julie's. But the actress asserts, "I definitely know girls like Marissa who can't stand their moms. She has a very controlling mom and it's difficult to try to live up to those expectations around her. She was raised to be a princess. But Marissa is not the kind of girl who is going to stay tied down. She doesn't want to be in Newport Beach for the rest of her life. I think when the show first started she was just taking a look at her surroundings and realizing it's not all it's cracked up to be."

always genuinely loved school. I like to learn," Mischa explains. "The school administration went to my parents and said I couldn't stay there and continue acting. They said I would never be able to get through school and act at the same time. I was so frustrated because I finally found something I loved to do and the school was telling me I couldn't."

Mischa's parents wanted her to be happy, so they began to look into other schools that would be more flexible with their daughter's acting pursuits. That's when they found The Professional Children's School. Most of the students there are involved in acting, music, or dance and need a flexible academic schedule. Actresses Christina Ricci and Scarlett Johansson went there. It was exactly what Mischa needed. "I was so happy to be around creative and artistic people who understood me better. I found my little niche," she says.

Balancing school and work became easier for Mischa, whose grades immediately improved because of this new arrangement. When she was in New York she would go to school every day. But if she was called away to work on a play or a movie, Mischa would take her lesson plans along and follow with the help of a hired tutor.

When Mischa was 11 she landed a leading role in an independent film called *Lawn Dogs*. Mischa was then offered a role as a sick child in the horror film *The Sixth Sense*, which starred Bruce Willis and Haley Joel Osment. "Even though my role was small, my character was very memorable. I was this little girl under a bed whose mother had this compulsive disease where she wants to poison her child. Everybody remembers that I threw up on Haley Joel Osment in my scene," Mischa says, laughing. "That movie gave my career a huge push."

The film was a huge success and Mischa's phone kept ringing with offers to do more films and television. She went on to land small roles in notable projects like the Julia Roberts movie *Notting Hill* and television's *Once and Again*.

Wanting to continue acting as much as she could, Mischa made a decision to accelerate her studies and earn her high school diploma by the age of 15. "I wanted to be able to work longer hours because it opens up the types of roles and the amount of work you're able to do at that age. In order to be in the big leagues with the adults you've got to work the adult hours and

Marissa's relationship with her dad, Jimmy (Tate Donovan), has been close.

either drop out of high school, which was not an option for me, or get a diploma," says Mischa, who still takes elective classes — for fun — from The Professional Children's School. "I love school. Now learning is fun as opposed to before when I was trying to cram it in during work."

A Star Is Born

Mischa was very happy with the balance she'd achieved between career and school. She was beginning to think about where she might want to go to college. Then, in the early spring of 2003, she got a call from her agent about a new television show called *The O.C.* Mischa jumped at the chance to audition. "This is the first character in my career where I get to play somebody my age," Mischa says of Marissa Cooper. "I have a lot of experience from high school that I base this character on. Since we're both 17 I feel very much a responsibility to keep her up-to-date with people I know around me and absorb that kind of behavior."

In many ways, Mischa and Marissa have a lot in common — besides their soundalike names! — and the producers of *The O.C.* picked up on this. Both girls are fans of young, hip designers like Zac Posen and Petro Zillia, both like to go shopping and meet friends for lunch, and both enjoy the same music. Oftentimes Mischa will pick up a script and see that Marissa will do or say something that Mischa says or does. For example, one day Mischa was having a conversation about music with fellow castmate Adam Brody. Josh Schwartz, *The O.C.* creator,

Marissa Cooper wonders where life will take her — Mischa Barton loves what she sees on the horizon.

overheard and took note. Soon after, says Mischa, "There was a scene in a car where we're talking about what kind of music we listen to and Marissa says she listens to punk. Then Seth starts making fun of her till she tells him she listens to the Clash and the Ramones. It's really funny because we totally had that conversation on set and Josh heard it all."

When she's not working, Mischa indulges her passion for music as often as she can. "One of my favorite things in the world to do is go to concerts. I go to as many as I can," she says, noting that she's gotten to meet some of her favorite bands, including members of The Strokes and Incubus.

Another of Mischa's favorite pastimes is reading. She has a huge collection of books, and it keeps growing. "I love to read. If I have a Saturday afternoon to myself I love going to the Barnes & Noble bookstore and buying some new CDs and reading," Mischa says.

Unlike her fellow castmates, who are older and live on their own in the Los Angeles area, Mischa shares a small rented house in Santa Monica with her mom while the show is shooting.

Her sister Hania and her father live in the family's New York home with Mischa's treasured pet, her cat, Angelo. Mischa's older sister, Zoe, is a barrister — the British equivalent of a trial lawyer — in London. When the occasional bout of homesickness creeps up on her, Mischa picks up the phone and gives Hania a call. They chat about school and the city and the show. "We're very close," Mischa says.

When the show takes a break, Mischa and her mom often travel back to New York to be with the family. In December, *The O.C.* shuts down production for two weeks so everyone can be with their real-life families for the holiday season. Mischa says those extended breaks are great because her family can take a vacation together. Last Christmas Mischa and her family vacationed in Italy for a week, then visited with relatives in Europe.

"My mom is from Ireland and my dad is from England," Mischa explains. "Half of my family lives one place and half of my family lives in the other, so we do try to get back a lot. I love to travel. It's one of my passions."

Boys & Beyond

Now that Mischa is a busy actress on a hit show, she's often invited to make appearances around the country. Last December she and the rest of her *O.C.* castmates attended the Billboard Music Awards in Las Vegas. Mischa regularly travels to New York to do publicity for the show, including magazine photo shoots (she's been on the covers of *Elle Girl*,

Will love last for Marissa and Ryan? It'll be a bumpy ride, but fans are definitely rooting for it.

Entertainment Weekly, *TV Guide,* and *Lucky*). When she's back home Mischa loves to jump into her favorite Calvin Klein jeans, hop on the subway with Hania, and shop for the afternoon in New York's trendy SoHo district.

"I have a sock obsession," Mischa confesses. "I get all kinds — ankle socks, leg warmers, knee socks. Striped socks are the best. I can't help myself."

Sock shopping is taking a backseat these days thanks to the success of *The O.C.* Beautiful Mischa was asked to be a spokesperson for Neutrogena beauty products and cosmetics. It was a huge honor for her to follow in the footsteps of other young Neutrogena spokesmodels like actresses Jennifer Love Hewitt and *Smallville* star Kristen Kreuk.

Last year Mischa branched out from *The O.C.* and shot a music video with Latin singing star Enrique Iglesias for his song "Addicted." Mischa played the girl Enrique couldn't get enough of. The two kissed throughout the video, which Mischa admits is pretty hot. "It's not easy making out with someone you've never met, but you just do it. Enrique is one of the nicest people I've ever met for someone in his position, which I think is pretty cool. We had a good time doing it."

Mischa also has a good time filming scenes — kissing or otherwise — with her *O.C.* costars because they've become so close. The bond the cast has formed over the past year actually helps them look more convincing as a group on the show. "There was a trial period of getting to know each other — like the first day of school. But now it feels like we're in such a groove, like we've known each other forever. Ben is so funny and down-to-earth. He makes it easy."

As for her own personal taste in boys, Mischa definitely sees the appeal of a Ryan Atwood type of guy. "I like rebellious boys. I definitely go for the more dark, brooding types. But I also like guys who are funny and smart and really intelligent."

Life is pretty great for Mischa, who says college is definitely in her future. "Nobody [in show business] really cares about you making room for it, but I definitely want to go to college someday," Mischa says, noting that Yale University is her top choice. "I come from a very academic family. My father studied law, politics, and economics and so did my sister (Zoe)."

SO YOU WANT TO BE A STAR?

Mischa knows she has one of the coolest jobs in the world. She gets to wear great clothes, travel around the country, and meet lots of famous people. But, she says, a career in acting isn't for everybody. Mischa's got three pieces of advice for those who think they might want to follow in her footsteps:

1. **BELIEVE IN YOURSELF.** "If you want something and you pursue it you can get it. You just have to know that you have it in you. If you really want to do it and you really feel you can, don't let somebody tell you you can't."

2. **ACTING IS FUN, BUT IT'S NOT EASY.** "You can't mind the long hours and the hard work. Something clicks and you know you want to do it because it makes you happy."

3. **IT'S NOT THE ONLY THING IN LIFE.** "You have to make sure you get an education alongside it. You don't want to be the one who drops out of school and doesn't have an education to fall back on."

Because she is committed to *The O.C.*, Mischa will defer enrolling in college for the time being, though she does continue to take elective literature, history, and writing courses through the The Professional Children's School.

"I look at my life right now as a blessing. I have this great job and I can take all these cool classes now that I might not have had time to do if I was in school full-time right now. Things get really hectic sometimes but I can't complain because I'm doing something I love to do."

THE BEAT ON BENJAMIN

FULL NAME: Benjamin McKenzie Schenkkan

NICKNAME: Ben ("growing up some people called me Bennie Mac")

BIRTH DATE: September 12, 1978

ASTROLOGICAL SIGN: Virgo

BIRTHPLACE: Austin, Texas

CURRENT RESIDENCE: Los Angeles

HAIR: Blond

EYES: Blue

HEIGHT: 5'9"

PARENTS: Pete Schenkkan, an attorney, and Frances Schenkkan, a poet/writer

SIBLINGS: Brothers Nate, 22, an actor, and Zack, 19, a student

HIGH SCHOOL: Austin High — Class of 1997

COLLEGE: University of Virginia — Class of 2001 (Bachelor's degree in Economics and Foreign Affairs).

BIG BREAK: *The O.C.*

FAVORITES

FOOD: Barbecue pork ribs

Watching college football or playing basketball

HOBBIES: Reading, running, hiking

SPORT: Football

TEAMS: University of Texas and Dallas Cowboys

ACTORS: Ed Norton, Russell Crowe, Sam Rockwell, Robert DeNiro, Al Pacino

ACTRESSES: Meryl Streep, Frances McDormand

MUSIC: Lyle Lovett, OutKast, Johnny Cash, Willie Nelson, Stevie Ray Vaughn

SNACK: Chocolate-covered espresso beans

ICE CREAM: Vanilla

MOVIES: *The Natural, Swingers, Dazed and Confused*

TV: Sports, *The West Wing*

HOLIDAY: Thanksgiving, "because it's football, food, and family. We have great family conversations around the dinner table and great food. It's a very relaxing day."

BOOK: *Empire Falls* by Richard Russo

AUTHORS: J. M. Coetzee and William Manchester

PET PEEVE: Mean-spiritedness, idiocy, or both together

WHAT HE LIKES IN A GIRL: Inquisitiveness, intelligence, sense of humor, ambition, and passion

WHAT HE DISLIKES IN A GIRL: Arrogance, manipulative game-players, taking too long to get ready, girls who don't eat on dates

HIDDEN TALENT: Cooks a mean pot of Texas-style chili

ALL ABOUT ADAM

FULL NAME: Adam Jared Brody

NICKNAME: Brody

BIRTH DATE: December 15, 1979

ASTROLOGICAL SIGN: Sagittarius

BIRTHPLACE: San Diego, California

CURRENT RESIDENCE: Hollywood

HAIR: Brown

EYES: Hazel

HEIGHT: 5'11"

PARENTS: Mark, an attorney, and Valerie, a graphic artist

SIBLINGS: 19-year-old twin brothers Sean and Matt (both in college)

PETS: "No. I have a plant."

HIGH SCHOOL: Scripps Ranch High School — Class of 1998

COLLEGE: Mira Costa Community College

BIG BREAK: *Gilmore Girls* — he played Lane's boyfriend

FAVORITES

FOOD: The "Matt Miller" sandwich at Canter's Deli in Los Angeles — roasted turkey on toasted challah bread with Muenster cheese, cole slaw, and Russian dressing

SPORTS: Surfing and basketball

ACTORS: Vince Vaughn, Ben Stiller, Owen Wilson, Matt Damon, Hugh Grant

ACTRESSES: Sandra Bullock, Julia Roberts

MUSIC: Bright Eyes, Ben Folds, Elliott Smith

SNACK: Veggies and fruit or cheese and crackers

VICE: Yogurt-covered pretzels

DESSERT: Cranberry oatmeal raisin cookies and vanilla ice cream

MOVIES: *About a Boy, Swingers, Batman*

TV: *The Daily Show*

HOLIDAY: "Halloween because it's the start of all the holidays. My favorite three months are October to December."

BOOKS: *The Amazing Adventures of Kavalier and Clay* by Michael Chabon, *Less Than Zero* by Bret Easton Ellis, *Catcher in the Rye* by J. D. Salinger

PET PEEVE: "Top 40 radio DJs drive me insane."

WHAT HE LIKES IN A GIRL: "She's gotta have a sense of humor and she's got to be confident and smart. It sort of goes hand in hand."

WHAT HE DISLIKES IN A GIRL: "I don't like someone who's too self-conscious."

A MINUTE WITH MISCHA

FULL NAME: Mischa Anne Marsden Barton

NICKNAME: Meesh or Meep

BIRTH DATE: January 24, 1986

ASTROLOGICAL SIGN: Aquarius

BIRTHPLACE: London, England

CURRENT RESIDENCE: New York City and Los Angeles

HAIR: Blond

EYES: Blue

HEIGHT: 5'8"

PARENTS: Paul, a broker, and Nula, a former photographer

SIBLINGS: Two sisters — Zoe, 26, a barrister (a lawyer in the traditional British court system, wears white wigs) — "I tease her about that constantly!" — and Hania, 15

PETS: Angelo, a cat

HIGH SCHOOL: The Professional Children's School in New York City

COLLEGE: She hopes to go to Yale University.

BREAKTHROUGH GIG: Mischa played a dying girl in the horror film *The Sixth Sense*.

FAVORITES

FASHION IDOLS: Cate Blanchett, Kate Beckinsale, Gwyneth Paltrow, Cameron Diaz

CLOTHING: Calvin Klein jeans

MUSIC: The Rolling Stones, The Beatles, The Strokes, Radiohead, Sum 41, Good Charlotte, U2, Coldplay

SNACK: Chocolate

BEAUTY PRODUCTS: Neutrogena's sesame body oil and Clarins lip balm

MOVIES: *Say Anything, Almost Famous, The Godfather, The Graduate*

TV: *The Simpsons, Saturday Night Live, CSI: Crime Scene Investigation,* and anything on Discovery Channel

HOLIDAY: Halloween and Christmas — "Both make you act like a kid again."

BOOK: *A Confederacy of Dunces* by John Kennedy Toole

AUTHORS: William Shakespeare, George Orwell

PET PEEVE: "I don't like messy people around me because I'm not great myself. I hate when people just throw stuff on the floor. I also hate wet socks — you know when you put on a fresh pair of socks and then you step in something wet? I hate that."

WHAT SHE LIKES IN A GUY: "Somebody who's open and understanding and intelligent. It's important to have depth. I like a man who's secure in who he is and is decisive."

WHAT SHE DISLIKES IN A GUY: "I don't like anybody fake."

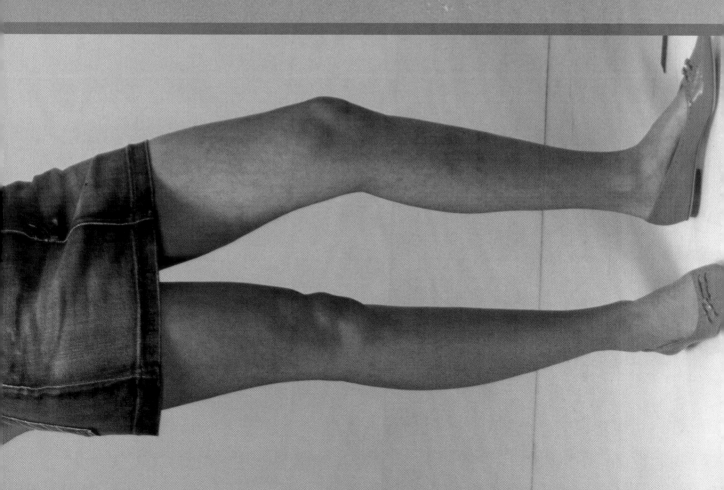

O.C. THE O.C. THE O.C. THE O.C. THE O.C. THE O.C. THE O.C. THE O.C. THE O.C.

O.C. THE O.C. THE O.C. THE O.C. THE O.C. THE O.C. THE O.C. THE O.C. THE O.

RACHEL BILSON
"SUMMER ROBERTS"

Rachel Bilson is Summer Roberts on *The O.C.* Summer is Harbor High's head socialite, the undisputed queen of what's in and what's "so yesterday." She's best friends with Marissa Cooper.

Summer's rep for getting whatever she wants, whenever she wants it, is well deserved. "I like to look at Summer as a go-getter," Rachel Bilson says of her character. "She's not always snobby."

Summer's turf is Newport Beach, and she thrives in that exclusive enclave. She loves fashion, adventure, and being in charge and in control — especially of her own emotions.

Seth Cohen was Summer's glitch. When the show began, Summer would not even consider giving Seth the courtesy of a hello. Halfway into the season, she began to acknowledge him. And fall for him! "Summer plays her games with Seth, but she's definitely into him," Rachel says.

Glitch number two was competition — but when Anna showed up, Summer awkwardly rose to the occasion by allowing herself to be vulnerable and admit her feelings to Seth, Marissa, Ryan, and Anna, a turn of events that Rachel applauds. "Summer has shown her layers a little bit and it's great because she doesn't act just one way. Nobody does."

Valley Girl

Rachel was born and raised in the San Fernando Valley section of Los Angeles.

Rachel received a firsthand look at how the entertainment business works via her dad, Danny Bilson, a writer, director, and producer who has worked on many movies and TV shows. "I grew up on sets so I guess you could say it's in the blood," Rachel explains. "I was always performing in some way, in talent shows or plays in school."

While a student at Notre Dame High School in Sherman Oaks, California, Rachel became very involved with the drama club and starred in productions like *Bye, Bye Birdie* and *Once Upon a Mattress*. During her senior year of high school, she decided to pursue an acting career.

"When I graduated I got an agent and started to go out on auditions," she says, noting that at the same time she had enrolled at Grossmont Community

In real life, Rachel's favorite designers are Marc Jacobs, Stella McCartney, and Chanel.

College in San Diego. "It was tough because I would have to drive so far to audition, so I wasn't as serious about acting because I was in college."

Only that didn't feel right. "I got to this point where I was, like, 'I gotta get serious and go for it.'" She moved back to Los Angeles so she could fully concentrate on building her career.

Several years and dozens of auditions later, Rachel's hard work paid off. She landed guest-starring roles on *8 Simple Rules for Dating My Teenage Daughter* and *Buffy The Vampire Slayer*.

Then Rachel was asked to audition for *The O.C.*

She felt confident during her audition. "I had a pretty good grasp on the role because I grew up in high school around girls who were a lot like Summer," Rachel says, noting that the audition process can be a little unnerving. "As an actor you go on so many auditions and you read for so many roles so you never think, 'Oh, I have this.' You never know. I was the first girl to read for the role of Summer, which is kind of cool. They asked me back four times and then I got it. Usually, being first wouldn't work to your advantage, but it did this time."

Star Turn

"A lot of people are surprised how nice I am," Rachel says of her fan encounters, which are a regular occurrence now that she's on a hit show. "Summer and I are both driven, but I'm not snobby. I'm a pretty good conversationalist and I like meeting new people."

On Saturday afternoons, Rachel's all about sleeping in, shopping, and lunching with friends.

In real life, she'd go for someone like Seth. "I like a guy who can make fun of me and make fun of himself. He's got to have a sense of humor," she says. "A guy can be the most beautiful thing in the world but if he opens his mouth and he's not interesting it won't work."

Since landing on *The O.C.* Rachel has become friends with her castmates, especially Mischa Barton and Samaire Armstrong. They chat about fashion and makeup and guys all the time. "I think it's important because it creates that chemistry on the show as well," Rachel says. "I can't imagine not getting along with them and having to work with them."

On weekends and days off Rachel likes to sleep in, catch a movie, or go shopping for vintage shoes and purses. "I collect them. Don't ask how many pairs of shoes I have — too many!" She laughs. "In my opinion you can never have enough shoes."

She also likes spending time (and money) on her two-year-old sister, Hattie. "Oh, my God. We had so many presents for her at Christmas," Rachel says. "I slept over with her and we were up at six A.M. It was so cool."

Rachel is often invited to Hollywood parties and awards shows where she gets to dress up in her favorite vintage and designer attire — and do face time with people whose work she admires. "I can handle myself pretty well, but I'm sure if Sean Penn was in front of me I'd just stand there, tongue on the floor, not knowing what to say."

Not being able to find the words isn't a regular occurrence for Rachel, who stays positive by following a simple philosophy. "I believe that everything happens for a reason," she explains. "If something happens that I don't necessarily agree with or I'm unhappy with I just remind myself to stay positive and trust that things happen the way they should. It really changed my life."

Rachel likes guys who have a sense of humor — like Adam's character, Seth.

THE RUNDOWN **ON RACHEL**

FULL NAME: Rachel Sarah Bilson
BIRTH DATE: August 25, 1981
ASTROLOGICAL SIGN: Virgo
BIRTHPLACE & CURRENT RESIDENCE: Los Angeles
PARENTS: Danny, a Hollywood writer/producer/director, and Janice, artist/counselor
SIBLINGS: Brother, John, 26, and sister, Hattie, 2
HAIR: Dark brown
EYES: Brown
HEIGHT: 5'2"
HIGH SCHOOL: Notre Dame High School — Class of 1999

FAVORITES
FOOD: Cereal. "I like all kinds — the healthy stuff and the not-so-good-for-you sweet stuff."
SNACK: Cookies
ICE CREAM: Cookies and Cream or Coffee
SPORT: Basketball

TEAM: Los Angeles Clippers
ATHLETE: Corey Maggette of the Los Angeles Clippers
ACTORS: Johnny Depp, Sean Penn, Christopher Walken
ACTRESSES: Sandra Bullock, Jennifer Aniston, Renee Zellweger and Brigitte Bardot
HOLIDAY: Halloween. "You get to dress up and it's fun to pretend."
MUSIC: Bruce Springsteen, Billie Holiday, Jeff Buckley
MOVIES: *Goonies, Welcome to the Dollhouse*
TV: *Friends, Sex and the City, The Golden Girls,* Shark Week on The Discovery Channel
BOOK: *Edie* by Jean Stein and George Plimpton
HOBBIES: Collecting vintage shoes and purses
PET PEEVE: "When you park in a parking lot and then you get out of your car and walk two spaces farther and there's a closer spot."
WHAT SHE DISLIKES IN A GUY: A name-dropper

CHRIS CARMACK
"LUKE WARD"

Chris Carmack plays Luke Ward, Harbor School athlete and Newport Beach golden boy. In many ways, Luke is like the "boy version" of Marissa Cooper — he seems to have it all, only to have it all unravel.

Tall, blond, blue-eyed, and buff, Luke's got money, popularity, and success as captain of the soccer and water polo teams at school. He's strong and sure of himself, the unopposed leader of the jock pack. If Luke often "solves" problems with his fists, well — as he famously snarled in the pilot episode — "That's the way it's done in *The O.C.*!"

Alas, it was Luke who came completely undone in the show's first season. He tumbled from his perch atop the high school food chain. His relationship with Marissa began to unravel with Ryan's arrival; any hopes of getting her back vanished when she caught him cheating. Being dumped was devastating, for underneath the bravado, Luke really loved Marissa. Luke's life took another unexpected and unwelcome turn when Luke caught his dad cheating on his mom — with another man.

The Luke character might have been a one-note bully whose comeuppance audiences would cheer. That he comes across as sympathetic is, in good part, due to the actor who plays him. In fact, Chris Carmack looks at Luke's lousy luck as a good thing!

"Luke's world is falling apart a little bit," explains Chris. "He was raised in a little bubble and he wasn't motivated to search outside that bubble because he was happy in it. These certain events force him to reexamine himself."

Luke was never a big fan of Seth Cohen's — less so when Seth brought Ryan into the picture.

Chris continues, "I think one of the reasons Luke never smiled and was always getting into fights is because he wasn't ever really happy. He had to repress elements of who he is to keep up that jock image. But nobody is cool all the time."

With his flaws and shortcomings revealed, Luke is now able to be more relaxed. He legitimately is a good guy deep down inside and he pays more attention to the good in other people. Now, says Chris, "Luke is going to be able to let loose a little bit more with people that accept him."

Chris is different from Luke when it comes to girls. "I've never been much of a Casanova. Dating was rough on me, though I have gotten better at it. I would never want to be 17 again," he says.

Luke is the boy Julie Cooper — Marissa's mom — would like her daughter to be seeing.

Born to Perform

James Christopher Carmack was born on December 22, 1980, to James, a businessman, and Susanne, an artist. He's called by his middle name to avoid family mix-ups with his dad. Chris was raised in Rockville, Maryland, with his older brother, Scott, now a stock trader, and a younger sister, Kate, a high school student.

As a young boy, Chris was into sports like baseball, basketball, and football. He loved playing in the neighborhood with all of his friends. Chris enjoyed meeting new people and was very outgoing and personable. He liked to make people feel comfortable and even more, make them smile. Chris admits, "I was a ham. I would turn an everyday conversation into a performance."

While attending Magruder High School, Chris excelled in basketball and wrestling. He also performed in school plays and musicals and was part of jazz and ensemble bands. That wasn't unusual at his school; there were no labels placed on the jocks or the drama students.

"There were students like me who were full-blown drama guys and were also on the sports teams," Chris says. "The drama club drew from all corners of the school. I convinced the guys from my team to come do the school musical. I was, like, 'It's fun and there's tons of hot girls doing it.'"

By the time Chris had graduated he had appeared in 15 shows and had participated in numerous theater and Shakespeare festivals. Still, Chris managed to study hard and get good grades. He decided to go to New York University, in part for its very reputable drama department. Chris quickly sponged up New York City culture, but found he wanted more, and opted to spend a semester in Italy. "I studied Italian, art renaissance history, and Italian cinema history through NYU for five months. I was pretty fluent, too," Chris says.

When Chris returned to New York he was referred to an agent who got him a job modeling for hip clothing company Abercrombie and Fitch. It was relatively easy work for Chris, who needed the money to support himself. But what he really wanted to do was act.

Chris left NYU after his sophomore year so he could move to Los Angeles to continue modeling and study acting. He landed a small role in the Comedy Central show *Strangers With Candy* in 2000, but it would be several more years of fruitless auditions before his next notable acting job.

Welcome to *The O.C.*, Dude

Being invited to audition for *The O.C.* was exciting, though Chris knew enough not to pin his hopes on it. But the first time he read Luke's lines, he connected with the material instantly. Personally, he was nothing like the character — "We look alike," he jokes, "but that's it" — but he'd known guys like Luke in high school, and drew from that experience. "It was a pretty smooth audition," Chris says. "I showed up and there were [only] two other guys there so I thought I had a decent shot. Sometimes you show up and there's ten guys reading for your part and you're like, 'Whoa!'"

His instincts were spot-on. Chris landed the part and has been having a blast ever since. "It's amazing to be a working actor, but to be a part of something that is so widely watched and embraced is even better," Chris says.

The O.C. had been on the air for a few months when Chris went home for Thanksgiving last year. That's when he found out his family are serious *O.C.* fans. "They love it. So many of my relatives watch[ed] it because I'm on it," Chris says. "When I was home they admitted to me whether I was on it or not they'd watch it. That's cool."

Chris's younger sister has been the most directly affected by her brother's stardom. "I know my sister is proud of me, but sometimes I think the show is more of a thorn in her side than a feather in her cap," Chris says, explaining that the show is all some of the kids at his sister's school want to talk about.

There's a wall between Marissa and Luke!

In his free time Chris can usually be found in his Santa Monica apartment writing music. He's an accomplished guitar and saxophone player and hopes to do some recording someday. Like his fellow *O.C.* castmates, Chris's own personality and tastes are slowly being reflected on the show. In one of the first season's episodes Luke played guitar and sang a song for Marissa and the gang, and it was actually a piece Chris wrote.

What does the future hold for Chris? He's not entirely sure, except that it will definitely involve acting, music, and traveling. "I haven't splurged on anything yet, but I'm hoping to buy a new computer and some music software," he says.

Chris also hopes to head back to Italy someday. "I first learned to chill out when I was living there. I want to see more of the world, too." Right now, though, Orange County suits Chris just fine.

CATCHING UP **WITH CHRIS**

FULL NAME: James Christopher Carmack
NICKNAME: Chris
BIRTHDATE: December 22, 1980
ASTROLOGICAL SIGN: Capricorn
BIRTHPLACE: Rockville, Maryland
CURRENT RESIDENCE: Santa Monica
HAIR: Blond
EYES: Blue
HEIGHT: 5'11"
PETS: Dog Hannah, Bichon and beagle mix (back home in Maryland)
HIGH SCHOOL: Magruder High School — Class of 1998
COLLEGE: New York University — left after sophomore year to pursue acting

FAVORITES

FOOD: Rotisserie chicken
SATURDAY AFTERNOON ACTIVITY: "I would drive over to my friend Scotty's house and play guitar all day."
SPORT: Baseball
TEAM: Baltimore Orioles
HOBBIES: Playing guitar and saxophone and writing music
COOKS: "I like to whip myself up an omelet when I'm hungry. I can grill steaks, too."
DESSERT: Pumpkin pie
ICE CREAM: Vanilla
ACTORS: Kevin Spacey, Jack Black
ACTRESSES: Cate Blanchett, Meryl Streep
MUSIC: Jazz and blues. "When I'm driving I like Muddy Waters or some old blues."
MOVIES: *Caddyshack, The Big Lebowski, What About Bob?*
TV: "I don't watch anything on TV, because my television only works with a VCR. I have to go to my friend's house to watch *The O.C.*"
HOLIDAY: "Thanksgiving because of all the great food, and that's when our family is all able to get together."
BOOKS: *The Fountainhead* by Ayn Rand and *A Portrait of the Artist as a Young Man* by James Joyce
PET PEEVE: "When people get angry about stupid stuff when they're driving — screamers. Just chill out!"
WHAT HE LIKES IN A GIRL: "I like girls who are smart, funny, and can hold their own in a conversation."
WHAT HE DISLIKES IN A GIRL: "A turnoff for me is a materialistic girl."

SAMAIRE ARMSTRONG

"ANNA STERN"

Samaire Armstrong is the talented actress who plays Harbor School newbie Anna Stern. Anna is the kind of girl most guys would want to date and get to know. She's beautiful, thoughtful, and kind, and unlike most of her *O.C.* peers, she likes people for who they are, and not what they can do for her. She is honest and open with her feelings, grounded, level-headed, and fairly unimpressed with her materialistic peers.

The only time she wasn't completely honest and open was with Seth. In her heart, Anna knew the quirky, quasi-dorky Seth was her soul mate, but she wasn't confident enough to go "up against" the vixen Seth was fixated on: Summer Roberts. Instead, Anna moved into the "best bud" position. That was short-lived, however; her real, romantic feelings came out soon enough. Bad timing, then, that Summer decided to return Seth's affections at the same moment. Vying for Seth's attention could have turned into a nasty game between Anna and Summer, but instead Anna urged Seth to choose. The ultimatum garnered Anna a lot of respect from both Seth and Summer.

Cut from the Same Cloth

People have taken notice of Samaire, too. Born in Tokyo, Japan, and raised in Sedona, Arizona, Samaire (pronounced SAW-ME-r̃a) learned early on that if she wanted something she'd have to work for — or on — it.

Her first lesson in "do-it-yourself" was about fashion. She enjoyed reading magazines and looking at what the models wore. She'd have loved to emulate those styles, but couldn't: "There were no malls [around where I lived]." Undeterred, Samaire went to Plan B: "I made all of my own clothes," she says proudly.

She developed her own funky style over the years, and still embraces non-mainstream fashion. "Vintage is my true love. Gap is great for T-shirts but I really don't believe in clothing for the masses," Samaire explains, noting that she and Anna tend to dress alike. "Our styles are almost weirdly similar — a little punky, lots of minis and studded bracelets. My dad has started calling me Samaire Stern."

As a student at Sedona's Red Rock High School, Samaire played varsity girl's volleyball for two years and dabbled in the drama club. Eventually, her love of acting trumped athletics, and Samaire had a career objective. After graduating, she enrolled in the University of Arizona. As a freshman, she couldn't wait to get involved with the drama department. Only she was rejected before she even got to meet anyone! The rejection wasn't personal: It was policy.

"In your freshman year there, you are not allowed to act in any of the productions, but they have all these rules to follow, like you have to help the older classmen get dressed and wash their clothes before and after plays — kind of like a fraternity or sorority," Samaire explains.

Samaire was undeterred. Again, she went to Plan B. "I was, like, why am I wasting my time here, why don't I just go out and do it? I came out to L.A. for the summer, and I never went back."

Samaire's unique look and natural talent quickly helped her land lots of television guest-starring roles on shows like *Party of Five, Freaks and Geeks, ER*, and *The X-Files*. She landed a breakthrough movie role as a conjoined twin in the comedy *Not Another Teen Movie*.

Her career was going along really well, still, Samaire couldn't believe it when she was asked to play Anna on *The O.C.* It turns out that Anna and Samaire have a similar fashion sense.

When Samaire isn't working she likes to go to fashion shows so she can check out what the industry's top designers unveil each season. Samaire plans to turn her childhood hobby of making clothes into a regular gig by unveiling her own fashion line someday.

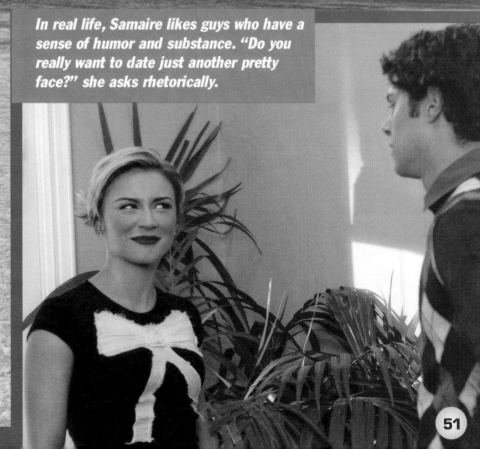

In real life, Samaire likes guys who have a sense of humor and substance. "Do you really want to date just another pretty face?" she asks rhetorically.

Adam Brody is "definitely boyfriend quality," Samaire says, though in real life, they are not dating.

During her free time she enjoys hanging out with friends, shopping, and grabbing a bite to eat. Sometimes she'll catch a band at a local club; other nights she's content to stay home. "Sometimes you're just so tired you want to light some candles and soak in a tub," she says. "That's pure heaven."

SAMAIRE STATS

HOMETOWN: Sedona, Arizona
CURRENT RESIDENCE: Los Angeles
BIRTHDATE: October 31, 1980
ASTROLOGICAL SIGN: Scorpio
HEIGHT: 5'5"
HAIR: Brown (currently dyed blond for *The O.C.*)
EYES: Brown
HIGH SCHOOL: Sedona Red Rock High School — Class of 1998

COLLEGE: University of Arizona

FAVORITES

CLOTHES: Vintage clothing
SNACK: Beef jerky, a mixture of milk and Hershey's baking chocolate, Splenda
TV: Old Clint Eastwood movies
BEAUTY PRODUCTS: Lotions and bubble baths. "I like any type of candy scent like vanilla or chocolate."

PETER GALLAGHER
"SANDY COHEN"

Peter Gallagher plays Sandy Cohen, a Newport Beach attorney who always sees the positive side of life and the good in his clients. Sandy champions the underdog.

That's because he relates. Sandy was just a poor kid from the Bronx who worked hard and graduated from Berkeley Law School. Now he's married to one of the wealthiest women in Orange County, lives in a mansion on a hill, and begins many a day with a little surfing in the Pacific Ocean before heading to work.

Somewhere along the line, someone gave Sandy a second chance: It's his mission to do the same for deserving others. Like Ryan Atwood. Even like Jimmy Cooper, his desperate neighbor who "used to be" — and still might be — in love with Sandy's wife, Kirsten.

Star Power

Peter Gallagher is the biggest star on *The O.C.* He's an award-winning Broadway stage actor and singer, a movie star, and now, the coolest — and best-looking — dad on TV.

Peter was born and raised in Armonk, New York, and became interested in drama during high school. While studying economics at Tufts University, Peter participated in community theater. In 1977 he made his professional debut in the hit musical *Hair*. He later went on to star in Broadway productions of *Grease* and *Guys and Dolls*.

His segue into films was just as successful. His most notable turns include *While You Were Sleeping, To Gillian on her 37th Birthday, American Beauty,* and *How to Deal.*

Jumping into a television series was a big deal for Peter, who wanted to make sure he was going to play a well-rounded character and not just some dad sitting at the dinner table. "I fell in love with the character," Peter says. "I liked the notion of playing an outsider, a guy from the Bronx, and I liked the notion of being a public defender."

There was more. "I loved the writing. I loved that there was a sense of humor to the show. People can take great delight in watching the rich fall on their face and the poor succeed."

Playing Sandy is comfortable for Peter because the two share some common traits. "I'm a New

Yorker, I am a liberal thinker, and I do believe in justice and fairness. I believe in people getting a chance," says Peter, who plans to follow in Sandy's footsteps and take up surfing this summer.

During his free time Peter enjoys golfing, swimming, and spending as much time as possible with his wife, Paula, and their two children — son Jamey, 13, and daughter Kathryn, 10. The family lives in New York while Peter films the show, though he does visit every other weekend during the season. "My son is a hockey player so I go to his practices and games and my daughter is a dancer so I go to her recitals."

Working on *The O.C.* has given Peter a great outlet for his talent, and a great new group of friends. "The kids — Ben, Adam, Mischa, Rachel, Chris, Samaire — I really care for them. I learn as much from them as they learn from me. They're real solid citizens, they have a great respect for acting and a desire to do it well. Plus, they're a lot of fun. I just like being with 'em."

To say that Peter is ecstatic about *The O.C.* is an understatement. "For an actor, if you have good words to say and people to listen to them, and good stories to tell, that's 90 percent of the battle," Peter says. "It's very exciting to be part of a show that you can be proud of."

KELLY ROWAN

"KIRSTEN COHEN"

Kelly Rowan plays Kirsten Cohen, *The O.C.*'s "supermom." Kirsten's got issues. Her dad never approved of her husband, and vice versa. She worries if she's a good mom to Seth — and she still has feelings for her former boyfriend, Jimmy Cooper. Kirsten's complicated, all right! Kelly Rowan, the beautiful actress who plays her, gets it! "She's a mom but she's a businesswoman and there's a price to pay when you're trying to juggle that."

North of the Border

Kelly Rowan was born in Ottawa, Canada, and raised in Toronto. She became interested in theater and after graduating from high school, she moved to New York City so she could study acting.

In 1990 she moved to Los Angeles, where she found instant success in film and television. She played Peter Pan's mother in the film *Hook* and guest-starred in TV shows like *CSI: Crime Scene Investigation* and *Boomtown*.

In her free time Kelly, who's single, enjoys traveling, reading, and writing. She's into a healthy lifestyle, and much like Kirsten, Kelly can regularly be found at the gym.

Kelly Rowan is proud of the show. "I love the writing on **The O.C.**, *and I love the character."*

TATE DONOVAN
"JIMMY COOPER"

Jimmy Cooper is played by actor Tate Donovan. Jimmy started the season at the top of his game — midway through, he'd fallen faster and harder than anyone else on the show. As a teenager Jimmy dated the richest, prettiest girl in town, Kirsten Nichol. But when the two went their separate ways for college, Kirsten met Sandy, and Jimmy met Julie: All fell in love and got married. He still, not-so-secretly, has feelings for Kirsten.

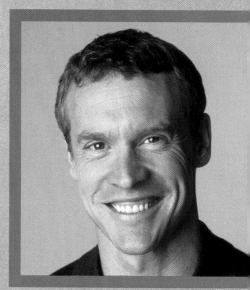

If that were only his biggest problem! An investment banker, he got into major debt by living well above his means. To keep up the facade for his wife and neighbors, he secretly dipped into his clients' savings plans to cover his bills.

Secrets are never kept very well on TV dramas, and Jimmy's exploded in his face — and in the faces of his wife, daughters, and entire community — when he was confronted by an enraged client during a huge social event.

Julie booted him and quickly hooked up with a real rich guy — Kirsten's dad! His friends dropped him. Only daughter Marissa stood by him, and even moved into his modest apartment for a while. With her support, as well as Kirsten and Sandy's, he is rebuilding himself and trying to regain the community's respect.

Tate Donovan understands his character well. "Jimmy starts at the bottom and he crawls his way back. He felt so much pressure living in that world and with that wife wanting to keep up with the Joneses. He buckled underneath the pressure but Jimmy learns his lesson and he makes a comeback."

Luck o' the Irish

Tate is the youngest of six children born and raised in Tenafly, New Jersey. When Tate was a teenager he became interested in acting and appeared in several TV shows. He was bitten by the bug, as they say in showbiz, and continued to pursue acting while studying theater at the University of Southern California.

In 1986 Tate landed a lead role in the movie *Space Camp*. It should have been a big break — only, in a classic case of bad timing, it was released shortly after the space shuttle *Columbia* crashed. "Nobody wanted to see a movie about space," Tate says.

He traveled back and forth between Los Angeles and New York doing TV, theater, films, and voice-over work. "Nothing I ever did was hugely popular," says a modest Tate, whose most memorable roles include recurring spots on TV's *Friends* and *Ally McBeal*. He also starred in the film *Love Potion No. 9* and was tapped to be the voice of Hercules in the Disney animated movie.

"To make a living as an actor is a major accomplishment," says Tate, who hopes to direct an episode of *The O.C.* next year. "I spend a lot of my time shadowing the director," Tate says.

In his free time Tate enjoys training for triathlons, rock climbing, white-water rafting, and playing the fiddle. "I play at [the restaurant] Finn McCool's in Santa Monica every Sunday. I play traditional Irish music." Tate is single and lives in Los Angeles.

MELINDA CLARKE
"JULIE COOPER"

Melinda "Mindy" Clarke plays Newport socialite Julie Cooper. Julie comes from modest means: Her one dream was to become wealthy. She realized that dream by marrying Jimmy Cooper and refused to give it up when Jimmy went belly-up.

Julie's antics may appear over-the-top at times, but the actress who gives her such sharp claws, Mindy Clarke, says there's more truth than fiction to her portrayal. "I grew up in Dana Point [the real Orange County!] and I've personally witnessed the kind of parties you see in that first episode. This is one side of life in Newport Beach that does exist. She [Julie] just does what she needs to do to keep up her status."

Like Father, Like Daughter

Mindy has a showbiz background. Her mom, Patricia, was a professional ballet dancer, and her father, John Clarke, starred on the TV soap *Days of Our Lives*. Growing up, Mindy studied theater and music. When she was 18 she landed a series regular role on her dad's show, *Days of Our Lives*. After three seasons, Mindy branched out and guest-starred in a variety of television shows, including *Xena: Warrior Princess, CSI: Crime Scene Investigation*, and *Everwood*. She also starred in musicals like T*he Music Man* and *West Side Story*. Her feature film credits include *Mullholland Falls* and *Spawn*.

Does playing calculating Julie make people think that Mindy is a nasty person in real life? "No one talks to me at work," Mindy jokes. Not at all! "Kelly Rowan and I get along together. I hang out with the girls. We went to the VH1 Awards and danced all night. And I have a little crush on Adam Brody."

In her free time Mindy enjoys singing and spending time with her family. She lives in Los Angeles with her husband, actor Ernie Mirich, and their two-year-old daughter, Kathryn.

BEHIND THE SCENES

People, Places . . . and Pranks!

Spending a day on the set of *The O.C.* is like a day at the beach. Well, almost. You can leave the sunscreen at home, since — spoiler alert #1 — most *O.C.* scenes are actually taped indoors. You know that spectacular view of the ocean from the window of the Cohen mansion?

A painted mural. And — spoiler alert #2 — they're not in Orange County.

The cast and crew report to *The O.C.* set at Raleigh Studios in Manhattan Beach, California, approximately 30 miles north of the sand and surf of Newport Beach. The same studio also doubles as Boston (*Boston Public* was filmed there) and Miami, as in *C.S.I.: Miami*.

But why not film on location, in the real Orange County? A bunch of reasons, mainly boiling down to time, money, convenience, and weather. Distance is a biggie. It's a long drive from Los Angeles, home base to the show's producers, directors, cast, and crew. The daily commute would take them along a freeway so jammed with traffic, it's actually referred to as Orange Crush.

Secondly, any time filming is done outside the facilities of a studio, expenses pile up: stuff viewers never think about, like production crews needing to obtain permits in order to film in public locations and the cost of transporting all the equipment to the location.

Then there's the unpredictable-weather factor. Sunny skies can suddenly become overcast and full of a misty drizzle. Which is a problem when the script calls for sun. *The O.C.*, like most TV series, needs to be filmed in a place where the lighting and temperatures can be controlled.

Big props, then, for the crew who do such an amazing job of replicating the Newport Beach scene that the casual viewer doesn't notice the difference. There was one exception, says *O.C.* creator Josh Schwartz. "Our lifeguard chairs are a different color than they are in Orange County. Somebody wrote in to tell us that. If that's our biggest problem then I can live with that."

Ben tries to brood like Ryan — but more often, says O.C.. boss Josh Schwartz, "He's a goofball."

57

THE O.C. TH THE O.C. THE O.C. THE O.C. THE O.C. TH
O.C. THE O.C.

The show is filmed inside soundstages, which are warehouse-size stucco buildings that are customized for whatever TV show or movie is using them. *The O.C.* uses soundstages 27 and 28 on the Raleigh lot. Soundstage 27 is called the "transitional" one, since the sets for scenes at the Harbor School, Crab Shack, Sandy's law office, and Kirsten's workspace can be interchanged.

Each of these sets looks normal enough on your TV screen, but behind the scenes, you can see that each "room" only has two or three walls: The rest of the space is filled with cameras and crew members, all of which is totally SOP (standard operating procedure) for TV shows or movies' interior scenes.

What's uncommon is Stage 28, which houses the Cohen family residence. It was modeled after a real mansion in Malibu, California. To make the Cohen household look as realistic as possible, the set designers built the home practically to scale. The rooms, the kitchen, the hallways, the backyard pool area, and the guest house where Ryan sleeps are all the actual size they would be in a real (really big!) home. The only major difference is that instead of an actual ceiling, dozens of cameras and lights are suspended from sturdy beams. The lights and cameras can be repositioned for each new scene.

For example, if there's a scene where Ryan and Seth are talking outside the pool house — which, remember, is actually shot indoors — the backyard still needs to look like it's actually outdoors. More than two dozen space lights — cylindrical lights encased in a white garbage-bag-like cover — illuminate the "yard." To give a sunlight effect, about a dozen rectangular 20K lights (very powerful 20-kilowatt lights) are positioned at an angle.

The pool is actually indoors.

To complete the illusion, several large round floor fans are positioned around the "backyard" set to create a gentle ocean breeze. So — spoiler alert #3 — that's not a natural breeze tossing Marissa's perfect tresses or weaving lazily through Seth's curls, it's a fan gently whirring in the background, which is also responsible for the swaying of the patio plants.

When shooting a scene that's supposed to be inside the house, the lights are turned up even brighter in the "outside" set, to give a contrasting effect. Sometimes the cameras film the actors indoors but catch glimpses of the backyard area. Because the outside scenery needs to look as realistic as possible, that's where the 25-foot mural of the ocean and neighboring houses comes in, hanging on a wall on the other side of the pool. Up close, it's completely obvious that it's a painting, but on camera it really does look like the Cohen household overlooks the ocean. And that's how it's done in *The O.C.*

Getting Pampered, Primped, and Primed for the Camera

Shooting a television show is a time-consuming process that requires extreme patience from both the cast and the crew. Everything has to be just right before the cameras start rolling. Not only do the set and the lights need to be in place, but the actors need to be camera-ready. In other words, the already gorgeous guys and gals need to get more gorgeous!

No bad hair days, no messy makeup, no shiny skin allowed for Cohens, Coopers, and cohorts. Being primped and pampered is one of the perks of the job.

Because the lights can sometimes be harsh, the actors' hair can't look too glossy, and their skin tones can't seem shiny. Special gels and sprays are used on their hair, and a makeup called pancake is applied to their faces.

Just like in real life, it takes the girls longer than the guys to get camera-ready, so Mischa, Rachel, Kelly, Samaire, and Melinda show up to work earlier than Ben, Adam, Peter, Tate, and Chris. Once makeup is applied and hair is in place, the actors put on the wardrobe selected for each scene.

What? You thought they wear their own clothes? Sorry — spoiler alert #4: Every outfit on each cast member — from

Chris Carmack as Luke, with director Ian Toynton.

A/X T-shirt to Pumas — is assembled by a talented wardrobe stylist, who knows each character's personality inside and out and gets to shop for them. Large racks, labeled by character, hang in the stylist's office. Kirsten, for example, might wear clothes from designers like Chanel or Prada while Marissa would likely wear Seven jeans or a Juicy Couture sweat suit.

All this precision is necessary to make sure the show and the characters look as authentic as possible. It takes time to get it all right. In general, each one-hour episode of *The O.C.* takes between five to seven days to film. An individual actor's day on the set can range from six to sixteen hours, depending on how many scenes that person is in and how many retakes end up happening.

"For every minute of footage [that you see on TV] there's probably 45 minutes of in-between time," Chris Carmack (Luke) explains. "That gives us a lot of downtime to deal with."

Dressing Room Downtime

Each actor has a personal dressing room located in a building adjacent to the sound-stages — that's where they spend what Chris refers to as "downtime." Each dressing room door is labeled by the *O.C.* character's name — not the actor's real name.

Inside they are all furnished identically, with a phone, a couch, a side table, and a coffee table. "It's so funny," Adam says. "All of the guys' rooms are so sparse and all of the girls did up their room like it's their home. The girls have blankets and pillows and candles and posters on the walls and my room looks like it did the day I got assigned to it."

Mischa agrees, laughing, "I've been trying to press Adam to decorate his room. He needs some serious help in there. It's beginning to look mildly depressing."

Mischa continues, "Rachel decorated hers and so did I. I have some Beatles and Rolling Stones and Clash posters. There's big cushions and candles and incense. I decorated my room with an eclectic mix of things I like to have around me and things I find comforting and soothing. I tend to read a lot or listen to music when I'm there."

Getting primped is part of the job!

Music is a common *O.C.* theme. On any given day you will hear several different kinds of music coming from the actors' rooms. Usually Ben is listening to Lyle Lovett or Willie Nelson while Rachel might have her stereo pumping out some hip-hop. Mischa likes to listen to faves like Radiohead once in a while, and Adam generally cranks out the latest tunes from his favorite indie bands. Chris makes his own tunes, practicing guitar in his room.

All of this activity is observed not-so-quietly by Josh and the other producers. Over the first season little bits of the cast's respective personal tastes and interests have found their way into *O.C.* scripts.

"I like to listen to what people

talk about," Josh says. "I try to make the actors feel as comfortable as possible with their characters because I hope they'll be playing them for a while. So if I hear somebody say something funny I try to put it in the show. Rachel and her friends all watch *The Golden Girls* together. They're each a different Golden Girl and I thought that was funny so in one of our episodes I had Summer and Anna bond over watching *The Golden Girls* and talk about which character they identify with. It's made them very guarded and wary around me."

The Munchies

During breaks, the cast often hits the "craft services" — Hollywood-speak for food — buffet table. The meals provided are generally easily prepared for the dozens of folks working on the set at any given time; usually sandwiches, salads, soups, and pastas are available. Throughout the day the cast can graze on healthy fare like fruit and fresh vegetables, or snack on not-so-healthy items like M&Ms and Red Vine licorice.

"Our set is really relaxed and friendly," Ben says. "We're not all working together on set all the time so it's sort of random groups of people at different times. We go to lunch together or some of the guys play music together on the set at lunch."

"You literally know how well your show is doing by how well the craft services table is stocked," Tate Donovan [Jimmy] says. "The first couple episodes the pickings are really slim. You get, like, a couple pieces of licorice and that's it. If the show's a hit you get Krispy Kreme doughnuts instead of some store brand. We're doing pretty well because they brought in these sandwiches called Thanksgiving sandwiches. You know how at midnight on Thanksgiving you go to the fridge and you're starving and you make a sandwich that has turkey, cranberry sauce, and stuffing and lettuce? Well, that's what we had and the crew went nuts. All work stopped when those sandwiches arrived."

Bonding — and Tattling — Like Family

Wonderland is the name of *O.C.* producer McG's production company. It could also be a way to describe the euphoric state the actors are in now that the show is a bona fide hit. As corny as it might sound, the cast has become very close.

"We really lucked out because none of us had met each other before we came to do this project," Mischa says. "People must think we look so dorky because we're hanging out together and we look like the lame-o cast from *The O.C.*"

Lame-o? Hardly, though Josh does have a few inside observations about the cast to share.

★ "Adam has never seen a movie he's liked."

★ "Ben is a total goofball — he tries to be brooding but he's pretty funny."

★ "Rachel is into Springsteen and Peter will sing show tunes at the drop of a hat." [Note: Peter Gallagher is an award-winning Broadway stage actor and singer — check out the cast album to the musical *Guys and Dolls*.]

★ "Tate is an extraordinary athlete and a true ladies' man."

★ "Melinda is much younger and nicer than her character."

★ "And Kelly, well, I would never eat any food that she eats — it's all this sort of wheat germ stuff."

"*I try to pick up a book as often as I can,*" Adam says.

Because most *O.C.* scenes are pretty intense, "There's not much time for us to joke and socialize during the workday," Mischa says.

Still, Adam finds a way to lighten things up. "Adam is always trying to make everyone laugh, which he does all the time. He's kinda like that little brother that's always making jokes in front of your parents. It's like you're supposed to be serious but you can't help yourself," Ben says. "Basically any time he does something funny we have to do two takes because the first time I laugh like crazy and the second time I know what's coming."

"We're really tight and we're all really good friends," Mischa says. "We had so much publicity stuff to do when the show first started so we were all together all the time."

The time together helped the cast bond tight friendships with one another early on. "We hang out, we go to parties or movies," Ben says.

And it's not just the young actors who have bonded.

"It's a different vibe here than other places I've worked," Adam says. "Everyone really gets along. I love Peter [Gallagher, who plays Sandy Cohen]. Everyone knows and loves Peter. I have the ultimate case of 'my dad is better than your dad' because I feel like he's the best. I think of him as sort of a father figure so when I see him and Kelly do a kissing scene it makes me feel kind of weird. I mean it's cool but yet I feel like I'm kind of watching my parents make out and it grosses me out."

"I really admire Peter," Ben says. "The thing I picked up from him right away is his attitude. He's humble and hardworking and friendly. He set the tone for the rest of the cast because he's the most accomplished name actor attached to the cast. He's been incredibly sweet so there's no room for the kids to be jerks."

But there's plenty of room for the kids to have fun. "This year the cast and I all went to a Halloween party," Mischa says. "I dressed like Catherine Zeta-Jones from *Chicago*, Adam dressed up as Ben Affleck, and Rachel was J-Lo. We had so much fun and we acted like kids. It was a good excuse to pretend we were somebody else for a night and a good excuse to fool around. Not that we need that."

> ## NEW WORDS *THE O.C.* HAS TAUGHT US:
>
> *Chrismukkah* — A combination of Christmas and Hanukkah
>
> *Yogalates* — A combo of yoga and Pilates

Rachel, Mischa, and Samaire often get together and go to the movies or go shopping and grab lunch. The guys Ben, Adam, Chris, and McG all play on the same entertainment basketball team. Every weekend they bond over a friendly game of hoops, though Ben admits their team isn't faring so well. "We are 1–3 right now. We definitely need the practice, especially Adam and me," Ben says. "Chris is really good. He's a natural athlete. We had to shoot a golfing scene on the show and neither of us had ever golfed before. I was barely hitting the ball 100 yards but Chris was crushing it. He was driving his ball 200 to 300 yards. He's gifted."

Presents and Pranks

Speaking of gifts, "We try to make a big deal out of birthdays, with cake and presents. Nobody's big day goes uncelebrated," says Mischa.

When Rachel turned 22 the group had a little celebration on the set. Adam is generally known as the wordsmith of the bunch with his quick and witty one-liners. But after Rachel's 22nd birthday, he's now known as the prankster.

"We were filming in the bio lab where there were real dead frogs for this scene where we were dissecting frogs," Mischa explains. "Rachel had a bunch of presents in her dressing room and —"

" — I took out the present I got her and put one of the dead frogs in the box," Adam picked up the story, "and then put her real gift in another box. So we all said good-bye when she left and she was carrying all her bags and she didn't know she had a dead frog with her. Then she got home and she was, like, showing her friends her gifts and she opened up the box where there's this dead frog. She was pretty freaked."

"She called me, screaming, 'We have to get Adam back!'" Mischa says, laughing. "We tried to get him back. We put fake blood on his dressing room door, but it didn't work. It's difficult because the boys are ruthless once they get going. They're always one step ahead of us."

Another prank involved Ben, Rachel, and Mischa. When the show airs, the cast often goes to McG's Hollywood Hills home to watch it together. One night Ben surprised the group with a little video he put together. Mishca remembers, "It had all of these embarrassing moments of Rachel and me on film. He had me in *Notting Hill* and *The Sixth Sense* and the clips were cut together to look really strange, like flashes in a weird music video. We all thought we were sitting down to watch an episode of the show together and everyone was waiting and suddenly this reel comes on."

"That kind of camaraderie makes it so much easier to work together," Mischa says.

Ben McKenzie sums it up best. "This show is amazing. It's like I've been handed this really great job and some people I can be friends with. How great is that?"

"This show is amazing. It's like I've been handed this really great job and some people I can be friends with. How great is that?"